CRYBABY

**To Alyse and Marc
and their firstborn, Olivia Hayley**

First Edition   1   2   3   4   5   6   7   8   9   10

Library of Congress Cataloging in Publication Data
Myers, Bernice. Crybaby/by Bernice Myers.
p.   cm. Summary: Michael joins the other members of his family in try-
ing to make his baby sister Sara stop crying. ISBN 0-688-09083-4. — ISBN 0-688-
09084-2 (lib. bdg.) [1. Babies—Fiction. 2. Brothers and sisters—Fiction.]
I. Title. PZ7.M9817Cr   1990   [E]—dc20
89-12342 CIP AC

Bernice Myers
CRYBABY

Lothrop, Lee & Shepard Books
New York

My name is Michael and
Sara's my baby sister.
She's new.
She can't talk yet.
But I like to play
with her.

"Why is Sara crying?"
my mother asks.

"Maybe she wants
to be
picked up,"
I say.

But Sara
keeps right on crying.

"I think
she wants to be
thrown
into the air,"
Dad says.

But Sara
keeps right on crying.

"Let's all make a
funny face.
Then Sara will
laugh,"
I say.
Dad thinks
my face
is the funniest.

But Sara
keeps
right
on
crying.

Grandpa
takes out his
watch
and jiggles it.
When I get bigger,
Grandpa's
going to give me
his watch.

Grandma
tickles Sara's stomach.
I show her my
favorite toy.

But Sara
keeps right on crying.

"Maybe she's hungry,"
Mom says.
"Maybe Sara
wants her bottle."

WOOF WOOF

"Maybe she wants to
play
with cat and dog,"
I say.

MEOWWW
WAAAAAA

"Maybe she wants
a fresh diaper,"
Grandpa says.

Grandma
has an idea.
"Maybe if we all sing,
Sara
will stop crying."

"Sara has a little lamb,
Little lamb, little lamb.
Sara has a little lamb,
Its fleece is white as snow...."

Everyone
is having fun
but
Sara.

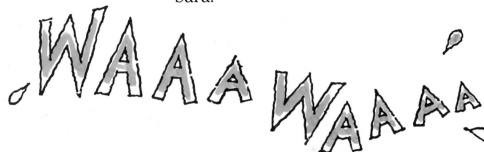

"What can
the matter be?"
Grandpa asks.

"Maybe something
hurts her,"
Grandma says.

"Maybe it's her
tummy,"
Dad says.

"Maybe she's SICK,"
I say.

"Then I'd better
call the doctor,"
Mom says.

We all wait
for the doctor to come.

"What?"
Mom says.

"Listen,"
I say.

Something must be wrong.
Everyone runs into
Sara's room.

"Look!
She's fast asleep,"
I say.

"That's all she wanted,"
Dad says.

Now Sara's awake again. I give her my finger to play with, and this time she can't stop laughing.